# Bibi *and* *the* Bull

Red Deer College Press

NORTHERN LIGHTS BOOKS FOR CHILDREN

**To my models**
Bibi – Paige Graham
Grandpa – Walter McBey
The Bull – Quantock (also known as Rhino)
The Landscape – Central Alberta in July
*–Thank you, Georgia Graham*

**To Krista**
The original "Bibi"
*–Carol Vaage*

*The Publishers*
Red Deer College Press
56 Avenue & 32 Street Box 5005
Red Deer Alberta Canada T4N 5H5

*Acknowledgments*
Financial support provided by the Alberta Foundation for the Arts, a beneficiary of the Lottery Fund of the Government of Alberta, and by the Canada Council and the Department of Canadian Heritage.

*Canadian Cataloguing in Publication Data*
Vaage, Carol, 1947–
Bibi and the bull
(Northern lights books for children)
ISBN 0-88995-178-0
I. Graham, Georgia, 1959– II. Title. III. Series.
PS8593.A13B52   1998   jC813'.54   C98-910859-7
PZ7.V13Bi   1998

*Publisher's Note:*
Bulls can be very dangerous animals, and parents and children are reminded to always exercise extreme caution.

Printed in Hong Kong for Red Deer College Press.

COMMITTED TO THE DEVELOPMENT OF CULTURE AND THE ARTS

THE CANADA COUNCIL | LE CONSEIL DES ARTS
FOR THE ARTS | DU CANADA
SINCE 1957 | DEPUIS 1957

5 4 3 2 1

# Bibi *and* *the* *Bull*

*Story by Carol Vaage*

*Illustrations by Georgia Graham*

Red Deer
College
Press

One summer, Bibi and her Mom went to stay at Grandpa's farm.
Grandpa took Bibi around the farmyard to show her the dangerous places.

He showed her the tractor.
He said, "Bibi, don't go near the tractor.
It's a big machine and you might get hurt."

He showed her the road.
He said, "Bibi, don't go near the road.
Big trucks roar by every day."

He showed her the pig pen.
He said, "Bibi, don't go in the pig pen.
Pigs are sloppy."

He showed her the chicken house.
He said, "Bibi, don't open the door to the chicken house.
All the chickens will fly out."

He showed her the barn.
He said, "Bibi, don't go in the barn.
The hay loft is dangerous and you might fall."

He showed her the bull pen.
He said, "Bibi, don't go in the bull pen.
The bull is big and mean and he will scare you."

So, Bibi played in the yard.   She played with her toys.   She played in the sandbox.
She played on the tire swing that Grandpa made.

Then one day, when Grandpa was in the barn,
and Mommy was in the house,
the bull got out of his pen
and walked over to Bibi.

He looked at Bibi.  Bibi looked at the bull.
He sniffed and snorted.  Bibi sniffed and snorted.

He pawed the ground with his hoof.
Bibi pawed the ground with her foot.

He raised his head and bellowed as loud as he could.
OW—OOO—OW—OOO!

Bibi raised her head and yelled as loud as she could.
III—EEE—III—EEE!

The bull was loud, but Bibi was louder!
Bibi's shriek was so loud
that it sent shivers straight down the bull's spine.

He jumped right up into the air,
then ran as fast as he could back into his pen!

Grandpa and Mommy could not believe their eyes.

The next time Grandpa took Bibi around the farmyard, he said:

"Bibi, don't go near the tractor. It's a big machine and you might get hurt.
Don't go near the road. Big trucks roar by every day.
Don't go in the pig pen. Pigs are sloppy.
Don't open the door to the chicken house. All the chickens will fly out.
Don't go in the barn. The hay loft is dangerous and you might fall."

When he got to the bull pen, he said,
"Bull, don't go in the yard.
Bibi is little but loud and she will scare you."

And the bull nodded his head, "YES!"

*Carol Vaage* is a kindergarten teacher who enjoys telling stories to her kids at home and at school. She well remembers the scary time when her own daughter had a run–in with a bull. Carol lives on an acreage near Edmonton, Alberta with (at last count) one husband, four kids, and 21 small animals. This is her first book — but not her last.

*Georgia Graham* loves to draw and she especially likes to illustrate children's books. She is a graduate of the Alberta College of Art. Georgia lives on a farm near Lacombe, Alberta with her husband, two kids, two horses, one dog, one cat, thirty–five cows and, of course, a bull. This is her third book — you'll be seeing her again.